カズオ・イシグロ
KAZUO ISHIGURO

土屋政雄訳

特急二十世紀の夜と、いくつかの小さなブレークスルー

ノーベル文学賞受賞記念講演

MY TWENTIETH CENTURY
EVENING
AND OTHER
SMALL BREAKTHROUGHS

THE NOBEL LECTURE

早川書房

カズオ・イシグロ

特急二十世紀の夜と、
いくつかの小さなブレークスルー

ノーベル文学賞受賞記念講演
2017年12月7日
ストックホルムにて

KAZUO ISHIGURO

My Twentieth Century Evening
and Other Small Breakthroughs

Nobel Lecture delivered
in Stockholm
on 7 December 2017

MY TWENTIETH CENTURY EVENING
AND OTHER SMALL BREAKTHROUGHS
by
Kazuo Ishiguro
Copyright © The Nobel Foundation 2017
Translated by
Masao Tsuchiya
First published 2018 in Japan by
Hayakawa Publishing, Inc.
Japanese translation published by
arrangement with
Kazuo Ishiguro c/o Rogers, Coleridge and White Ltd.
through The English Agency (Japan) Ltd.

装幀：早川書房デザイン室

The Nobel Prize in Literature for 2017 is awarded to Kazuo Ishiguro "who, in novels of great emotional force, has uncovered the abyss beneath our illusory sense of connection with the world".

——The Swedish Academy

2017年ノーベル文学賞はカズオ・イシグロ氏に授与される。氏は「強く感情に訴えかける数々の小説により、世界との結びつきという錯覚の下に口を開ける奈落を描き出してみせた」。

——スウェーデン・アカデミー

My Twentieth Century Evening and Other Small Breakthroughs

If you'd come across me in the autumn of 1979, you might have had some difficulty placing me, socially or even racially. I was then twenty-four years old. My features would have looked Japanese, but unlike most Japanese men seen in Britain in those days, I had hair down to my shoulders, and a drooping bandit-style moustache. The only accent discernible in my speech was that of someone brought up in the southern counties of England, inflected at times by the languid, already dated vernacular of the hippie era. If we'd got talking, we might have discussed the Total Footballers of Holland, or Bob Dylan's latest album, or perhaps the year I'd just spent working with homeless people in

特急二十世紀の夜と、いくつかの小さなブレークスルー

　1979年の秋に私を見かけた人は、さて、これはどんな社会階層の男だろう、と首をひねったかもしれません。人種さえよくわからないな、と。私は24歳でした。顔形は日本人だったでしょうが、当時のイギリスで見かけるほとんどの日本人男性とは違っていたはずです。両肩まで伸びた髪に、端の垂れ下がった山賊スタイルの口髭。言葉は、イングランド南部諸州の訛りがわずかに感じられる程度で、普通の英語。ただしときおり、もう時代遅れになりつつあった、気怠いヒッピー話法が混じっていたかもしれません。私に声をかけてくれる人がいれば、オランダのトータルフットボールのこと、ボブ・ディランの最新アルバムのこと、ロンドンでホームレスの人々と過ごしてきたばかりの1年のことなどを話題にできた

London. Had you mentioned Japan, asked me about its culture, you might even have detected a trace of impatience enter my manner as I declared my ignorance on the grounds that I hadn't set foot in that country – not even for a holiday – since leaving it at the age of five.

That autumn I'd arrived with a rucksack, a guitar and a portable typewriter in Buxton, Norfolk – a small English village with an old water mill and flat farm fields all around it. I'd come to this place because I'd been accepted on a one-year postgraduate Creative Writing course at the University of East Anglia. The university was ten miles away, in the cathedral town of Norwich, but I had no car and my only way of getting there was by means of a bus service that operated just

でしょう。しかし、その人がもし日本に言及し、かの国の文化のことなどを尋ねてきたら、私はきっと、それは5歳のとき離れた国で、以後は休暇の旅行でさえ行ったことがなく、何も知らない、と答えたはずです。そう答える私の態度には、かすかな苛立ちさえ見てとれたかもしれません。

　その秋、私はリュックを背負い、ギターとポータブルタイプライターをぶら下げて、ノーフォーク州バクストンに到着しました。イングランドの小さな村で、古い水車場があり、その周囲に平らな農地が広がっています。なぜそんなところに来たかと言えば、イーストアングリア大学大学院の創作科という1年間の課程に受け入れてもらえたからでした。大学自体はノリッチという町にあります。大聖堂で知られた町で、バクストンからは10マイルも離れています。私には車がありませんでしたか

once in the morning, once at lunchtime and once in the evening. But this, I was soon to discover, was no great hardship: I was rarely required at the university more than twice a week. I'd rented a room in a small house owned by a man in his thirties whose wife had just left him. No doubt, for him, the house was filled with the ghosts of his wrecked dreams – or perhaps he just wanted to avoid me; in any case, I didn't set eyes on him for days on end. In other words, after the frenetic life I'd been leading in London, here I was, faced with an unusual amount of quiet and solitude in which to transform myself into a writer.

In fact, my little room was not unlike the classic writer's garret. The ceilings sloped claustrophobically

ら、ノリッジにはバスで行くしかありません。朝に１本、昼食時に１本、夕方にもう１本。日に３本だけのバスでした。しかしすぐに、大学には週にせいぜい２日ほど顔を出せばよいことがわかり、大した問題にはなりませんでした。小さな家に部屋を１つ借りました。大家さんは30代の男の人で、奥さんに出ていかれたばかりだとのことでした。大家さんにとっては、挫折した夢の亡霊が宿る家だったのでしょうか、それとも私を避けたかっただけでしょうか、何日も連続して姿を見かけないことがよくありました。こうして、ロンドンで目が回るような日々を送っていた私は、一転、ありあまるほどの静けさと孤独の中に移り住み、作家への変身を目指すことになったわけです。

　実際、私の小さな部屋は、「作家の屋根裏部屋」という古典的な通念とさほど違わなかったでしょう。天井の

– though if I stood on tip-toes I had a view, from my one window, of ploughed fields stretching away into the distance. There was a small table, the surface of which my typewriter and a desk lamp took up almost entirely. On the floor, instead of a bed, there was a large rectangular piece of industrial foam that would cause me to sweat in my sleep, even during the bitterly cold Norfolk nights.

It was in this room that I carefully examined the two short stories I'd written over the summer, wondering if they were good enough to submit to my new classmates. (We were, I knew, a class of six, meeting once every two weeks.) At that point in my life, I'd written little else of note in the way of prose fiction, having earned my place on the course with a radio play

傾斜は閉所恐怖症を誘いそうなほどでしたが、爪先立ちすれば、1つだけの窓から外が覗け、耕された畑が遠くまで広がっているのが見えました。小さなテーブルは、タイプライターと卓上スタンドを置くと、ほぼいっぱいになりました。床にはベッドがなく、かわりに長方形の大きな工業用フォームが置いてありました。ここに寝ると、寒さの厳しいノーフォークの夜にさえ寝汗をかくほどでした。

　その部屋で、夏に書き上げておいた2つの短篇を丹念に読み直しました。クラスは総勢6人、2週間に1度ずつ集まると聞いていました。はたして新しいクラスメートに読んでもらうに足る作品だろうか……。あのときまで、私は散文小説などほかにあまり書いたことがなく、創作科への願書に添えたのも、BBCに送って突き返されてきたラジオドラマでした。とにかく20歳までにロ

rejected by the BBC. In fact, having previously made firm plans to become a rock star by the time I was twenty, my literary ambitions had only recently made themselves known to me. The two stories I was now scrutinising had been written in something of a panic, in response to the news that I'd been accepted on the university course. One was about a macabre suicide pact, the other about street fights in Scotland, where I'd spent some time as a community worker. They were not so good. I started another story, about an adolescent who poisons his cat, set like the others in present-day Britain. Then one night, during my third or fourth week in that little room, I found myself writing, with a new and urgent intensity, about Japan – about Nagasaki, the city of my birth, during the last days of the Second World War.

特急二十世紀の夜と、いくつかの小さなブレークスルー

ックスターになるという計画があって、それにこだわっていましたから、自分に文学への野心があることに気づいたのさえ、さほどまえのことではありません。あの部屋で読み直していた２つの短篇は、創作科に受け入れてもらえることがわかってから、半ばパニック状態で書いたものでした。１つは陰気な心中の話、もう１つは、スコットランドでコミュニティワーカーとして働いた経験を下敷きにした路上喧嘩の話です。いくら読み直しても、いい出来とは言えません。もう１つ書くことにしました。今度は猫を毒殺しようとする思春期の少年の話で、まえの２篇同様、現代イギリスを舞台にしました。ですが……ある夜のことです。その部屋に住みはじめて３週目か４週目のことだったでしょうか。不意にこれまでにない差し迫った思いにとりつかれ、気がつくと、私は日本について──生まれた町、長崎について──第２次世界大戦の終戦間際の話を書きはじめていました。

This, I should point out, came as something of a surprise to me. Today, the prevailing atmosphere is such that it's virtually an instinct for an aspiring young writer with a mixed cultural heritage to explore his 'roots' in his work. But that was far from the case then. We were still a few years away from the explosion of 'multicultural' literature in Britain. Salman Rushdie was an unknown with one out-of-print novel to his name. Asked to name the leading young British novelist of the day, people might have mentioned Margaret Drabble; of older writers, Iris Murdoch, Kingsley Amis, William Golding, Anthony Burgess, John Fowles. Foreigners like Gabriel García Márquez, Milan Kundera or Borges were read only in tiny numbers, their names meaningless even to keen

特急二十世紀の夜と、いくつかの小さなブレークスルー

　私自身にも、あれは驚きでした。いまの世なら、多文化的な背景をもつ若者が作家を目指すとき、作品の中で自分の「ルーツ」を探るのはいわば本能的な行為とすら言えます。しかし、当時の状況はまったく違っていました。イギリスで「多文化主義」の文学が勃興するのは、何年か先のことです。サルマン・ラシュディは、まだ、絶版になった小説が1冊あるだけの無名作家でした。有望な若手イギリス人作家をあげろと言われたら、人々はマーガレット・ドラブルをあげたかもしれません。上の世代の作家なら、アイリス・マードック、キングズリー・エイミス、ウィリアム・ゴールディング、アンソニー・バージェス、ジョン・ファウルズといったところでしょうか。外国人作家を読むのはごく限られた人々で、ガブリエル・ガルシア゠マルケス、ミラン・クンデラ、ボルヘスなどは、熱心な読書家にとってさえとくに意味の

readers.

Such was the literary climate of the day that when I finished that first Japanese story, for all my sense of having discovered an important new direction, I began immediately to wonder if this departure shouldn't be viewed as a self-indulgence; if I shouldn't quickly return to more 'normal' subject matter. It was only after considerable hesitation that I began to show the story around, and I remain to this day profoundly grateful to my fellow students, to my tutors, Malcolm Bradbury and Angela Carter, and to the novelist Paul Bailey – that year the university's writer-in-residence – for their determinedly encouraging response. Had they been less positive, I would probably never again have written about Japan. As it was, I returned to my

ない名前でした。

　当時の文学的空気がそんなものでしたから、日本をテーマにした最初の短篇を書き終えたとき、私は何か新しい方向、進むべき重要な方向を見つけたと感じました。しかし、強くそう感じた直後に、疑いが忍び込みました。新しい方向などと、自分勝手な思い込みではないのか。もっと「普通」のテーマにさっさと戻るべきではないのか……。ずいぶんためらってから、ようやくその短篇を周囲にも見せる決心をしました。クラスメート５人、指導教師のマルカム・ブラッドベリーとアンジェラ・カーター、あの年の大学逗留作家だったポール・ベイリーには、今日にいたるまで深い感謝の念でいっぱいです。あの方々が、あの作品に明確に好意的な反応を示してくれなかったら──励ましに本気が感じられなかったら──おそらく、私が日本について書くことは２度となかった

room and wrote and wrote. Throughout the winter of 1979-80, and well into the spring, I spoke to virtually no one aside from the other five students in my class, the village grocer from whom I bought the breakfast cereals and lamb kidneys on which I existed, and my girlfriend, Lorna (today my wife), who'd come to visit me every second weekend. It wasn't a balanced life, but in those four or five months I managed to complete one half of my first novel, *A Pale View of Hills* – set also in Nagasaki, in the years of recovery after the dropping of the atomic bomb. I can remember occasionally during this period tinkering with some ideas for short stories not set in Japan, only to find my interest waning rapidly.

でしょう。私は屋根裏部屋に戻り、必死で書きつづけました。1979-80年の冬とそれにつづく春、ほとんど誰とも口をきかずに書いていたと思います。例外は、クラスメートと、村の食料品店の主人（なにしろ、この店で買う朝食用シリアルと子羊の腎臓で生き延びたようなものですから）、そして隔週末に訪ねてくるガールフレンドの（現在の妻の）ローナだけでした。とてもバランスのとれた生活とは言えませんが、とにかく４、５カ月もその生活をつづけ、最初の長篇小説である『遠い山なみの光』の半分を書き上げました。やはり長崎を舞台とし、原爆投下後の復興の時期を描いた小説です。この期間中、日本以外をテーマにした短篇小説のアイデアもいくつか浮かび、あれこれいじってみましたが、いざやりはじめると、どれもこれも急速に書く気が失せていったのを覚えています。

Those months were crucial for me, in so far as without them I'd probably never have become a writer. Since then, I've often looked back and asked: What was going on with me? What was all this peculiar energy? My conclusion has been that just at that point in my life, I'd become engaged in an urgent act of preservation. To explain this, I'll need to go back a little.

*

I had come to England, aged five, with my parents and sister in April 1960, to the town of Guildford, Surrey, in the affluent 'stockbroker belt' thirty miles south of

特急二十世紀の夜と、いくつかの小さなブレークスルー

　私にとって決定的に重要な数カ月でした。あの時期がなかったら、たぶん作家にはなっていなかったでしょう。あのとき私に何が起きていたのか——ときどき振り返っては自問しました。あの異様なエネルギーは何だったのか……。私の人生において、何かを緊急に保存することが必要になっていた一時期、というのが私の得た結論です。それをおわかりいただくためには、少し過去にさかのぼらなければなりません。

＊

　1960年4月、5歳の私は両親に連れられ、姉とともにイギリスにやってきました。落ち着いた先はロンドンから南へ30マイルほどのところにあるサリー州ギルフォ

London. My father was a research scientist, an oceanographer who'd come to work for the British government. The machine he went on to invent, incidentally, is today part of the permanent collection at the Science Museum in London.

The photographs taken shortly after our arrival show an England from a vanished era. Men wear woollen V-neck pullovers with ties, cars still have running boards and a spare wheel on the back. The Beatles, the sexual revolution, student protests, 'multiculturalism' were all around the corner, but it's hard to believe the England our family first encountered even suspected it. To meet a foreigner from France or Italy was remarkable enough – never mind one from Japan.

ード、俗に「ストックブローカー・ベルト」と呼ばれている高級住宅地の一つです。父は、イギリス政府に招かれた海洋学研究の科学者でした。ちなみに、ロンドンの科学博物館に行けば、父が後に発明した機械が常設展示物の一つになっています。

　到着して間もないころに撮った写真には、いまではもう見られないイギリスが写っています。男はＶネックのウールのプルオーバーを着てネクタイをし、車はまだランニングボードを備えて、後部にスペアタイヤを背負っています。ビートルズ、性革命、学生の抗議行動、多文化主義……すべてがすぐそこまで迫っていましたが、私の家族が初めて接したイギリスには、そんなことの予感すらなかっただろうと思わされます。日本人はもちろん、フランス人やイタリア人さえ見かけることがまれな時代でした。

Our family lived in a cul-de-sac of twelve houses just where the paved roads ended and the countryside began. It was less than a five-minute stroll to the local farm and the lane down which rows of cows trudged back and forth between fields. Milk was delivered by horse and cart. A common sight I remember vividly from my first days in England was that of hedgehogs – the cute, spiky, nocturnal creatures then numerous in that country – squashed by car wheels during the night, left in the morning dew, tucked neatly by the roadside, awaiting collection by the refuse men.

All our neighbours went to church, and when I went to play with their children, I noticed they said a small prayer before eating. I attended Sunday school, and

特急二十世紀の夜と、いくつかの小さなブレークスルー

　私たち一家は、12軒の家が立ち並ぶ袋小路に住んでいました。舗装された道路が終わって田園が始まるあたりで、近くの農場までは歩いて5分もかかりませんでしたし、野原から野原へ移動する牛の行列が小道を行き来しているのをよく見かけました。牛乳配達には馬車が使われていました。イギリスに来た直後によく目にして、いまでも鮮明に覚えているのは、ハリネズミのいる光景です。当時の田舎には、針のような毛で覆われたこの夜行性のかわいい動物が数多くいて、よく夜中に車にひきつぶされ、朝露の中に転がっていました。道路脇にそっと除(の)けられ、ゴミ収集人による回収を待っていました。

　隣近所の住人はみな教会に通っていました。友達の家に遊びにいくと、食事のまえにみなで短いお祈りをしていて、そうするものなのかと知りました。私も日曜学校

before long was singing in the church choir, becoming, aged ten, the first Japanese Head Chorister seen in Guildford. I went to the local primary school – where I was the only non-English child, quite possibly in the entire history of that school – and from when I was eleven, I travelled by train to my grammar school in a neighbouring town, sharing the carriage each morning with ranks of men in pinstripe suits and bowler hats, on their way to their offices in London.

By this stage, I'd become thoroughly trained in the manners expected of English middle-class boys in those days. When visiting a friend's house, I knew I should stand to attention the instant an adult wandered into the room; I learned that during a meal I had to ask permission before getting down from the table. As the

に行きました。やがて教会の聖歌隊で歌うようになり、10歳のときには、ギルフォード初の日本人聖歌隊長になりました。通っていた地元の小学校では、私がただ1人の外国人生徒でした。ひょっとしたら、小学校創設以来初めての外国人生徒だったかもしれません。11歳になると隣町のグラマースクールに行くようになり、毎朝、大人に交じって汽車で通学しました。大人たちはロンドンのオフィスで働く人々で、ピンストライプのスーツを着て、山高帽をかぶっていました。

　当時のイギリス中産階級の少年に求められていた行儀作法というものも、このころの私はしっかりマスターしていました。たとえば、友人の家を訪れたとき、大人がふらりと部屋に入ってきたら、さっと立ち上がって気を付けの姿勢をとることも、食事中にテーブルから離れるには、必ず許可をもらわなければならないことも、知っ

only foreign boy in the neighbourhood, a kind of local fame followed me around. Other children knew who I was before I met them. Adults who were total strangers to me sometimes addressed me by name in the street or in the local store.

When I look back to this period, and remember it was less than twenty years from the end of a world war in which the Japanese had been their bitter enemies, I'm amazed by the openness and instinctive generosity with which our family was accepted by this ordinary English community. The affection, respect and curiosity I retain to this day for that generation of Britons who came through the Second World War, and built a remarkable new welfare state in its aftermath, derive significantly from my personal experiences

ていました。近隣でただ1人の外国人の少年である私は、地元で一種の有名人でした。子供たちは、出会うまえから私のことを知っていましたし、通りを歩き、店で買い物をしていると、ときに、まったく見知らぬ大人から名前で呼ばれることもありました。

　第2次世界大戦が終わって、まだ20年も経っていないころのことです。その大戦では日本がイギリスの憎い敵だったはずです。当時を振り返ってそんなことを思うとき、イギリスのごく普通のコミュニティが自然な寛大さで私たち一家を迎え入れ、分け隔てなく接してくれたことに感銘すら覚えます。大戦をくぐりぬけ、その後にすばらしい新福祉国家を築いたあの世代のイギリス人に、私は今日まで愛情と敬意と好奇心を抱きつづけています。そんな気持ちのかなりの部分は、子供のころの個人的体験によって形作られたものでしょう。

from those years.

But all this time, I was leading another life at home with my Japanese parents. At home there were different rules, different expectations, a different language. My parents' original intention had been that we return to Japan after a year, perhaps two. In fact, for our first eleven years in England, we were in a perpetual state of going back 'next year'. As a result, my parents' outlook remained that of visitors, not of immigrants. They'd often exchange observations about the curious customs of the natives without feeling any onus to adopt them. And for a long time the assumption remained that I would return to live my adult life in Japan, and efforts were made to keep up the Japanese side of my education. Each month a

特急二十世紀の夜と、いくつかの小さなブレークスルー

　一方、家の中の私は、日本人である両親のもとで外とはまったく別の生活をしていました。内には外と異なるルールがあり、異なる期待があり、異なる言語がありました。もともと、両親は1年か、場合によったら2年で日本に帰るつもりでいました。イギリスに来て最初の11年間、私たちは常に「来年」帰るつもりでいたと言ってよいでしょう。その結果、両親の心にある未来は、定住者のそれではなく、単なる訪問者のそれのままでした。よくイギリス人の奇妙な習慣を見ては感想を述べ合っていましたが、その習慣を自分たちも受け入れねばならなくなるとは感じていなかったようです。私の成人後の生活は日本にあるというのが最初からの前提で、そのための教育も忘れられてはいませんでした。毎月、日本から小包が届きました。中身は月遅れの漫画や雑誌、教育的

parcel arrived from Japan, containing the previous month's comics, magazines and educational digests, all of which I devoured eagerly. These parcels stopped arriving sometime in my teens – perhaps after my grandfather's death – but my parents' talk of old friends, relatives, episodes from their lives in Japan all kept up a steady supply of images and impressions. And then I always had my own store of memories – surprisingly vast and clear: of my grandparents, of favourite toys I'd left behind, the traditional Japanese house we'd lived in (which I can even today reconstruct in my mind room by room), my kindergarten, the local tram stop, the fierce dog that lived by the bridge, the chair in the barber's shop specially adapted for small boys, with a car steering wheel fixed in front of the big mirror.

なダイジェスト本などで、私はそのすべてを貪(むさぼ)るように読みました。10代のいつごろからか——たぶん、祖父が死んでからでしょう——小包は来なくなりました。それでも、両親が旧友や親戚について話すこと、日本での生活の中で起こったあれこれについて話すことを聞いていましたから、私の中に流れ込む日本のイメージや印象が途絶えることはありませんでした。もちろん、私自身の頭に蓄積された記憶もあります。驚くほど大量で明確な記憶でした。祖父母のこと、家に残してきたお気に入りのおもちゃのこと、住んでいた伝統的な日本家屋のこと（いまでも心の中で家全体の間取りを再現できます）、幼稚園のこと、路面電車の停留場のこと、橋の近くに飼われていた猛犬のこと……。床屋さんには小さな子供用に改造された椅子があって、大きな鏡のまえに自動車のハンドルが取り付けられていたのも覚えています。

What this all amounted to was that as I was growing up, long before I'd ever thought to create fictional worlds in prose, I was busily constructing in my mind a richly detailed place called 'Japan' – a place to which I in some way belonged, and from which I drew a certain sense of my identity and my confidence. The fact that I'd never physically returned to Japan during that time only served to make my own vision of the country more vivid and personal.

Hence the need for preservation. For by the time I reached my mid-twenties – though I never clearly articulated this at the time – I was coming to realise certain key things. I was starting to accept that 'my' Japan perhaps didn't much correspond to any place I

そんな生活の結果、何が起こったか。成長するにつれ、私の心の中に「日本」という名の特異な場所が作り上げられていったということです。虚構の世界を文章で書こうなどと思いつくずっと以前から、「日本」という、なぜか私の属する場所であり、私に自信とアイデンティティの感覚を与えてくれる場所が、精緻に作られつづけていました。実際の日本には１度も戻っていませんでしたが、それだけに、心に作られる日本はいっそう鮮明になり、私だけの国になっていったように思います。

　だからこそ保存が必要でした。20代半ばに達するころの私は、明確に意識することはなくても、ある重要な事実に気づきはじめていたのだと思います。つまり、「私の」日本は、たぶん、現実に飛行機で行けるどの場所とも一致していないだろうということ。両親の話から

could go to on a plane; that the way of life of which my parents talked, that I remembered from my early childhood, had largely vanished during the 1960s and 1970s; that in any case, the Japan that existed in my head might always have been an emotional construct put together by a child out of memory, imagination and speculation. And perhaps most significantly, I'd come to realise that with each year I grew older, this Japan of mine – this precious place I'd grown up with – was getting fainter and fainter.

I'm now sure that it was this feeling, that 'my' Japan was unique and at the same time terribly fragile – something not open to verification from outside – that drove me on to work in that small room in Norfolk. What I was doing was getting down on paper that

想像でき、私自身の幼いころの記憶にもある暮らしぶりは、1960年代から70年代にかけてほとんど消え失せているだろうということ。そもそも、私の頭の中にある日本は、子供が記憶と想像と憶測から作り上げた感情的産物にすぎないのかもしれないということ……。私はそのことを認めはじめていました。そして、たぶん最も重要なのは、年々歳をとっていくにつれ、「私の」日本が――私が身近に感じながら成長してきたこの貴重な場所が――しだいに薄れゆきつつあると気づいたことです。

　私はいま確信しています。「私の」日本という特異な場所はひどく脆い。外部からの検証を許さない。そんな感覚があって、それがノーフォークのあの小部屋で私を駆り立てたのだと思います。私がしたことは、あの場所の特別な色彩や風習や作法、その荘重さや欠点など、そ

world's special colours, mores, etiquettes; its dignity, its shortcomings, everything I'd ever thought about the place, before they faded forever from my mind. It was my wish to re-build my Japan in fiction, to make it safe, so that I could thereafter point to a book and say: 'Yes, there's my Japan, inside there.'

*

Spring 1983, three and a half years later. Lorna and I were now in London, lodging in two rooms at the top of a tall narrow house, which itself stood on a hill at one of the highest points of the city. There was a television mast nearby and when we tried to listen to records on

の場所について私が考えていたすべてを、心から永久に失われてしまわないうちに紙に書き残すことでした。私は自分の日本を小説として再構築し、安全に保ちたかったのでしょう。今後はいつも１冊の本を指差して、「そう、この中に私の日本があります」と言えるように。

＊

　３年半後の1983年春。ローナと私はロンドンにいて、あるひょろ長い建物の最上階にある２部屋を借りて住んでいました。建物自体が、ロンドンで最も高い地域にある丘の上に立っていて、近くにテレビ塔があり、そのせいか、部屋でレコードをかけようとすると、得体の知れ

our turntable, ghostly broadcasting voices would intermittently invade our speakers. Our living room had no sofa or armchair, but two mattresses on the floor covered with cushions. There was also a large table on which I wrote during the day, and where we had dinner at night. It wasn't luxurious, but we liked living there. I'd published my first novel the year before, and I'd also written a screenplay for a short film soon to be broadcast on British television.

I'd been for a time reasonably proud of my first novel, but by that spring, a niggling sense of dissatisfaction had set in. Here was the problem. My first novel and my first TV screenplay were too similar. Not in subject matter, but in method and style. The more I looked at it, the more my novel resembled a screenplay –

ない放送音が断続的にスピーカーに入り込んできたりしました。居間にはソファも安楽椅子もなく、ただ床に２枚のマットレスを敷いて、その上にクッションを散らしてありました。大きなテーブルが１つあって、昼間は私がそこで書き物をし、夜は２人でそこで食事をしました。豪華さとは程遠くても、私たち２人はそんな暮らしが気に入っていました。私は前年に最初の小説を出版していたほか、短篇ドラマの脚本も書いていて、それがテレビで間もなく放送されることになっていました。

　出版した最初の小説のことは、当初、まずまず誇らしく思っていました。しかし、この春になるころには小さな不満を覚えるようにもなっていました。何が問題だったかと言えば、同じく初めて書いたテレビドラマの脚本に似すぎてはいないかということです。テーマはともかく、手法やスタイルが似ていて、見れば見るほど脚本の

dialogue plus directions. This was okay up to a point, but my wish now was to write fiction that could work properly *only on the page*. Why write a novel if it was going to offer more or less the same experience someone could get by turning on a television? How could written fiction hope to survive against the might of cinema and television if it didn't offer something unique, something the other forms couldn't do?

Around this time, I came down with a virus and spent a few days in bed. When I came out of the worst of it, and I didn't feel like sleeping all the time, I discovered that the heavy object, whose presence amidst my bedclothes had been annoying me for some time, was in fact a copy of the first volume of Marcel Proust's

ような、対話とト書きで成り立っているような小説に思えてきました。ある程度はかまわないでしょう。ですが、当時の私は、ページに印刷されて初めて本領を発揮する小説を書きたいと思っていました。本を読んでも、テレビをつけたときと同様の体験しかできないなら、わざわざ小説として読む意味がないのではないか。小説にしかできない何か、他の媒体には不可能な何かを提供できないなら、強力な映画やテレビを相手に小説はどうやって生き残れるだろう……？

　ちょうどこのころ私はウイルスにやられ、何日か寝込むはめになりました。最悪期を脱し、もう寝てばかりいるのにうんざりしてきたとき、しばらくまえから寝具の中に紛れ込んでいて気になっていた何か重いものが、マルセル・プルーストの『失われた時を求めて』の第１巻であることに気づきました。せっかく手元にあるのだか

Remembrance of Things Past (as the title was then translated). There it was, so I started to read it. My still fevered condition was perhaps a factor, but I became completely riveted by the Overture and Combray sections. I read them over and over. Quite aside from the sheer beauty of these passages, I became thrilled by the means by which Proust got one episode to lead into the next. The ordering of events and scenes didn't follow the usual demands of chronology, nor those of a linear plot. Instead, tangential thought associations, or the vagaries of memory, seemed to move the writing from one episode to the next. Sometimes I found myself wondering: Why had these two seemingly unrelated moments been placed side by side in the narrator's mind? I could suddenly see an exciting, freer way of composing my second novel; one that

特急二十世紀の夜と、いくつかの小さなブレークスルー

らと思い、手に取って読みはじめました。きっと、まだ熱が抜けきっていなかったせいもあったのでしょうか、すっかり「序章」と「コンブレー」の虜になり、何度も何度も読み返しました。単純に文章が美しかったこともありますが、それ以上に、1つのエピソードを次のエピソードへつなげていくプルーストのやり方に身震いするほど興奮したからだと思います。この作品では、出来事や場面の流れが通常の時間の流れに従っていません。直線的な話の筋にも従っていません。そうではなく、いわば連想の脱線や記憶の気まぐれが推進力となって、話を次から次へつないでいきます。ときどき、はてなと考え込まされることがあります。あの瞬間とこの瞬間は一見無関係と思えるのに、なぜ語り手の心の中では隣り合うように存在しているのだろうか……。突然、目のまえに、私の2冊目の小説への取り組み方が開けてきました。これまでより自由で、胸躍るような方法です。この方法な

could produce richness on the page and offer inner movements impossible to capture on any screen. If I could go from one passage to the next according to the narrator's thought associations and drifting memories, I could compose in something like the way an abstract painter might choose to place shapes and colours around a canvas. I could place a scene from two days ago right beside one from twenty years earlier, and ask the reader to ponder the relationship between the two. In such a way, I began to think, I might suggest the many layers of self-deception and denial that shrouded any person's view of their own self and of their past.

*

ら本の各ページを豊かにし、スクリーンでは捉えようのない内的な動きを読者に示せるのではないか。もし、語り手の思考の流れや記憶の漂流に従って話を展開していけるなら、ちょうど抽象画家がキャンバス上に形や色を配置していくように文章を書けるのではないか。2日前の出来事を20年前の出来事のすぐ隣に置き、両者の関係に注意を向けるよう読者を促すこともできるのではないか。そういう書き方なら、人が自らや自らの過去を理解しようとするとき、その理解を十重二十重（とえはたえ）に覆って曇らせている自己欺瞞や否認の存在を暗に示せるのではないか……。私はそんなことを考えはじめました。

＊

March 1988. I was thirty-three years old. We now had a sofa and I was lying across it, listening to a Tom Waits album. The previous year, Lorna and I had bought our own house in an unfashionable but pleasant part of South London, and in this house, for the first time, I had my own study. It was small, and didn't have a door, but I was thrilled to spread my papers around and not have to clear them away at the end of each day. And in that study – or so I believed – I'd just finished my third novel. It was my first not to have a Japanese setting – my personal Japan having been made less fragile by the writing of my previous novels. In fact my new book, to be called *The Remains of the Day*, seemed English in the extreme – though not, I hoped, in the manner of many British authors of

特急二十世紀の夜と、いくつかの小さなブレークスルー

　1988年3月。わが家にはいまソファがあって、33歳の私はそのソファに寝転がり、トム・ウェイツのアルバムを聴いていました。じつはまえの年、ローナと私は南ロンドンに家を買っていました。時流からは少し取り残された地域ながら、住みやすい場所にある家でした。その家で、私は初めて書斎なるものをもつことができました。ドアもない小さな部屋でしたが、原稿をいくら散らしておいてもよく、毎晩片づけずにすむというのは、やはり感動ものです。その書斎で、私は3作目となる小説を書き終えたばかりでした（終えた、と思っていました）。前2作で私の日本を保存できたこともあり、3作目『日の名残り』は、日本を舞台としない初めての小説となりました。むしろ、逆にきわめてイギリス的な小説と言えるかもしれません。ただ、その「イギリス的」は、上の世代の多くの作家に見る「イギリス的」とは意味合いが

the older generation. I'd been careful not to assume, as I felt many of them did, that my readers were all English, with native familiarity of English nuances and preoccupations. By then, writers like Salman Rushdie and V.S. Naipaul had forged the way for a more international, outward-looking British literature, one that didn't claim any centrality or automatic importance for Britain. Their writing was post-colonial in the widest sense. I wanted, like them, to write 'international' fiction that could easily cross cultural and linguistic boundaries, even while writing a story set in what seemed a peculiarly English world. My version of England would be a kind of mythical one, whose outlines, I believed, were already present in the imaginations of many people around the world, including those who had never visited the country.

違うと私は思って――願って――います。たとえば、上の世代の方々は、読者がすべてイギリス人であって、英語のニュアンスやイギリス人の関心事に精通していることを前提としていたように思いますが、私は意識的にその前提を避けてきました。このころにはすでにサルマン・ラシュディやＶ・Ｓ・ナイポールが現れ、もっと国際的で外向きの視線をもつイギリス文学が台頭してきていました。つまり、イギリス中心主義に立たず、イギリス重視を当然としない文学です。この人々の作品は、ごく広い意味でポストコロニアル的と言えるでしょう。私もまた彼らのように書きたいと思いました。たとえ舞台がきわめてイギリスらしい世界だとしても、私の物語には、文化的・言語的な境界を容易に越えていく「国際性」をもってほしいと思いました。私の書くイギリスは、一種神話的なイギリスとなるでしょう。そういうイギリスのおおよその姿形は、現実のイギリスをまだ訪れたことの

The story I'd just finished was about an English butler who realises, too late in his life, that he has lived his life by the wrong values; and that he's given his best years to serving a Nazi sympathizer; that by failing to take moral and political responsibility for his life, he has in some profound sense wasted that life. And more: that in his bid to become the perfect servant, he has forbidden himself to love, or be loved by, the one woman he cares for.

I'd read through my manuscript several times, and I'd

ない人々も含め、世界中の人々の想像力の中にすでに存在している、と私は信じました。

*

　私が書き終えたばかりの物語は、イギリス人執事の話です。彼は誤った価値観によって人生を誤ったと悟りますが、すでに遅しです。執事として、人生最良の年月をナチ・シンパの主人に捧げてきました。自分の人生なのに、自分で道徳的・政治的責任を負わずにきたことによって、人生をいわば無駄にしたことを深く悔やみます。それだけではありません。完璧な召使いであろうとするあまり、大切に思う１人の女性がいながら、それを愛し、それに愛されることを自らに禁じます。

　私は書き上げた原稿を何度も読み返して、まずまず満

been reasonably satisfied. Still, there was a niggling feeling that something was missing.

Then, as I say, there I was, in our house one evening, on our sofa, listening to Tom Waits. And Tom Waits began to sing a song called 'Ruby's Arms'. Perhaps some of you know it. (I even thought about singing it to you at this point, but I've changed my mind.) It's a ballad about a man, possibly a soldier, leaving his lover asleep in bed. It's the early morning, he goes down the road, gets on a train. Nothing unusual in that. But the song is delivered in the voice of a gruff American hobo utterly unaccustomed to revealing his deeper emotions. And there comes a moment, midway through the song, when the singer tells us that his heart is breaking. The moment is almost unbearably moving

足していました。同時に、何かが足りないという小さな思いを抑えられずにいました。

　そして、ある夜のことです。申し上げたとおり、私は家のソファに寝転がり、トム・ウェイツを聴いていました。「ルビーズ・アームズ」という歌が始まりました。この歌をご存じでしょうか（じつはこの場で歌ってみることも考えたのですが、やはりやめておきましょう）。ある男を歌ったバラードです。兵士かもしれません。眠る恋人をベッドに残し、立ち去ろうとしています。時刻は早朝。男は道を下り、汽車に乗ります。特別な内容ではありません。ですが、ウェイツの声が特別です。アメリカ人放浪者のしわがれ声で——深い感情を明かすことなどしたことがない声で——歌っています。歌が進み、やがて中ほど、心が張り裂けそうだと歌う瞬間が来て、聞き手はほとんど堪えきれないほどの感動を覚えます。

because of the tension between the sentiment itself and the huge resistance that's obviously been overcome to declare it. Tom Waits sings the line with cathartic magnificence, and you feel a lifetime of tough-guy stoicism crumbling in the face of overwhelming sadness.

As I listened to Tom Waits, I realised what I'd still left to do. I'd unthinkingly made the decision, somewhere way back, that my English butler would maintain his emotional defences, that he'd manage to hide behind them, from himself and his reader, to the very end. Now I saw I had to reverse that decision. Just for one moment, towards the end of my story, a moment I'd have to choose carefully, I had to make his armour crack. I had to allow a vast and tragic yearning to be

張り裂けそうな感情それ自体と、それを言葉にするまでに乗り越えねばならなかったはずの強い抵抗の壁……両者間の緊張から来る感動でしょう。トム・ウェイツが歌うこの1行のすばらしさは、聞き手にカタルシスをもたらします。圧倒的な悲しみをまえに、タフガイを貫いてきた男のとりつくろった平静さが崩れ去るのを感じます。

　トム・ウェイツを聴いて、私は何をやるべきかを悟りました。イギリス人執事には最後まで感情の防壁を維持してもらい、その防壁によって自分からも読者からも自分自身を隠しきってもらう……。書いている途中のどこかで、私は無意識にそう決めていたのだと思います。いまやるべきことは、その無意識の決定を覆すことです。物語の終わりに近いどこかで、一瞬だけ覆そう。その一瞬を慎重に決め、まとった鎧に一筋のひび割れを起こさせよう。鎧の下にある大きくて痛ましい願いを、読者に

glimpsed underneath.

I should say here that I have, on a number of other occasions, learned crucial lessons from the voices of singers. I refer here less to the lyrics being sung, and more to the actual singing. As we know, a human voice in song is capable of expressing an unfathomably complex blend of feelings. Over the years, specific aspects of my writing have been influenced by, among others, Bob Dylan, Nina Simone, Emmylou Harris, Ray Charles, Bruce Springsteen, Gillian Welch and my friend and collaborator Stacey Kent. Catching something in their voices, I've said to myself: 'Ah yes, that's it. That's what I need to capture in that scene. Something very close to that.' Often it's an emotion I can't quite put into words, but there it is, in the singer's

垣間見てもらおう。

　私はこれまで、いくつもの場面で、歌手の歌声から重要なことを学んできました。歌われる歌詞からもそうですが、実際の歌唱から学ぶことが多かったように思います。ご存じのとおり、歌うときの人間の声は、計り知れないほど複雑に絡み合った感情でも表現できるものです。これまでの長い年月に、私の文章はいくつもの面で多くの歌手から影響を受けてきました。何人か例をあげれば、ボブ・ディラン、ニーナ・シモン、エミルー・ハリス、レイ・チャールズ、ブルース・スプリングスティーン、ジリアン・ウェルチ、そして私の友人であり合作者でもあるステイシー・ケントといった方々です。その人々の歌唱から何かを感じたとき、私は自分に「そう、これだ」と言います。「あの場面にこれを――これに近い何かを――取り込まねば……」と。それは、言葉では表現

voice, and now I've been given something to aim for.

*

In October 1999, I was invited by the German poet Christoph Heubner on behalf of the International Auschwitz Committee to spend a few days visiting the former concentration camp. My accommodation was at the Auschwitz Youth Meeting Centre on the road between the first Auschwitz camp and the Birkenau death camp two miles away. I was shown around these sites and met, informally, three survivors. I felt I'd come close, geographically at least, to the heart of the dark force under whose shadow my generation had

しきれない感情ですが、歌手の歌声にはちゃんとあって、私は目指すべき何かをもらったと感じます。

*

　1999年10月、ドイツの詩人クリストフ・ホイプナーを通じて、国際アウシュビッツ委員会から強制収容所跡の見学に招待されました。アウシュビッツ青年集会所を宿舎とし、数日かけての見学ということでした。この集会所は、アウシュビッツ第1収容所と、そこから2マイル先のビルケナウ死の収容所の中間にあります。2つの収容所跡を案内してもらい、非公式ながら3人の生存者の方々と面会しました。そのとき、私たち世代の成長過程にまで影を落としつづけた暗黒の力の中核に、確かに——少なくとも地理的に——近づいたことを感じました。

grown up. At Birkenau, on a wet afternoon, I stood before the rubbled remains of the gas chambers – now strangely neglected and unattended – left much as the Germans had left them after blowing them up and fleeing the Red Army. They were now just damp, broken slabs, exposed to the harsh Polish climate, deteriorating year by year. My hosts talked about their dilemma. Should these remains be protected? Should Perspex domes be built to cover them over, to preserve them for the eyes of succeeding generations? Or should they be allowed, slowly and naturally, to rot away to nothing? It seemed to me a powerful metaphor for a larger dilemma. How were such memories to be preserved? Would the glass domes transform these relics of evil and suffering into tame museum exhibits? What should we choose to remember? When is it

特急二十世紀の夜と、いくつかの小さなブレークスルー

　雨の午後に訪れたビルケナウのガス室跡は、瓦礫化していました。赤軍から逃げようとしてドイツ軍がここを爆破したままに——ほとんどそのままに——残されているそうです。手入れもなく放置されている様が不思議でした。いまでは湿り気を帯びたコンクリート片の山となり、ポーランドの厳しい気候にさらされて、年々朽ちていっています。招待者の方々は、ジレンマを抱えていると話してくれました。風防ガラスのドームで覆い、後世の目にも触れるよう残すべきなのか、それとも自然に、徐々に、朽ち果てていくのに任せるべきなのか。私には、その悩みがもっと大きなジレンマの暗喩(あんゆ)のように聞こえました。こうした記憶はどう保存すべきなのか。ガラスのドームで覆うことで、悪と苦痛の遺物が博物館の穏やかな展示物に変わってしまうのか。私たちは何を記憶するかをどう選択したらいいのか。忘れて先へ進んだほうがいいと、いつ言えるのか……。

better to forget and move on?

I was forty-four years old. Until then I'd considered the Second World War, its horrors and its triumphs, as belonging to my parents' generation. But now it occurred to me that before too long, many who had witnessed those huge events at first hand would not be alive. And what then? Did the burden of remembering fall to my own generation? We hadn't experienced the war years, but we'd at least been brought up by parents whose lives had been indelibly shaped by them. Did I, now, as a public teller of stories, have a duty I'd hitherto been unaware of? A duty to pass on, as best I could, these memories and lessons from our parents' generation to the one after our own?

特急二十世紀の夜と、いくつかの小さなブレークスルー

　私は44歳でした。そのときまで、第２次世界大戦というものは、数々の恐怖や勝利の話ともども両親の世代のこと、と考えていました。しかし、いま、この巨大な出来事をじかに体験した人々が遠からずいなくなる、と思い当たりました。そのあとはどうなるのだろう。記憶しておくという責務が、私たちの世代に引き継がれるのだろうか。私たち自身は戦争の年月を体験していませんが、その私たちを育てた両親の世代は、否応なく人生に戦争を刻み込まれています。物語を公に語る者である私は、いままで気づかずにいたけれど、その責務を引き継ぐ立場にあるのではないか。両親の世代の記憶と教訓を、できるだけ力を尽くして、次に来る世代に伝える義務があるのではないか……。

A little while later, I was speaking before an audience in Tokyo, and a questioner from the floor asked, as is common, what I might work on next. More specifically, the questioner pointed out that my books had often concerned individuals who'd lived through times of great social and political upheaval, and who then looked back over their lives and struggled to come to terms with their darker, more shameful memories. Would my future books, she asked, continue to cover a similar territory?

I found myself giving a quite unprepared answer. Yes, I said, I'd often written about such individuals struggling between forgetting and remembering. But in the future, what I really wished to do was to write a story about how a nation or a community faced these

特急二十世紀の夜と、いくつかの小さなブレークスルー

　その後しばらくして、東京で講演をする機会がありました。集まった人々の中から、次はどんな作品を？　という質問が出ました。よくある質問です。しかし、この方の質問は、もう少し詳しく言うとこんな具合でした。まず、私の小説には、社会的・政治的に大きな混乱の時期を生きた人の物語が多いと指摘し、その人物は自分の人生を振り返り、暗く恥ずべき記憶となんとか折り合いをつけようとする、と前置きして、これからもそういう物語を書いていくのですか、と尋ねました。

　私の答えは、自分でもまったく思いがけないものでした。はい、と答えました。これまで、忘れることと記憶することの間で葛藤する個人を書いてきたが、これからは、国家や共同体がこの問題にどう向き合うかをテーマに書いていきたい、と。国家も、個人と同じように記憶

same questions. Does a nation remember and forget in much the same way as an individual does? Or are there important differences? What exactly are the memories of a nation? Where are they kept? How are they shaped and controlled? Are there times when forgetting is the only way to stop cycles of violence, or to stop a society disintegrating into chaos or war? On the other hand, can stable, free nations really be built on foundations of wilful amnesia and frustrated justice? I heard myself telling the questioner that I wanted to find a way to write about these things, but that for the moment, unfortunately, I couldn't think how I'd do it.

*

したり忘れたりするものなのか。それとも、そこには重要な違いがあるのか。国家の記憶とは、いったいどんなものなのか。それはどこに保存されているのか。どうやって作られ、どう管理されているのか。暴力の連鎖を断ち切り、社会が混乱と戦争のうちに崩壊していくのを阻止するためには、忘れる以外にないという状況もありうるのか。としても、意図的な健忘症と挫折した正義を地盤として、その上にほんとうに自由で安定した国家を築くことなどできるのか。私はそういうことについて書く方法を見つけたいが、残念ながら、いまのところどうやっていいかわからずにいる……。私の耳に、そんなことを質問者に答えている自分の声が聞こえてきました。

*

One evening in early 2001, in the darkened front room of our house in North London (where we were by then living), Lorna and I began to watch, on a reasonable quality VHS tape, a 1934 Howard Hawks film called *Twentieth Century*. The film's title, we soon discovered, referred not to the century we'd then just left behind but to a famous luxury train of the era connecting New York and Chicago. As some of you will know, the film is a fast-paced comedy, set largely on the train, concerning a Broadway producer who, with increasing desperation, tries to prevent his leading actress going to Hollywood to become a movie star. The film is built around a huge comic performance by John Barrymore, one of the great actors of his day. His facial expressions, his gestures, almost every line he

特急二十世紀の夜と、いくつかの小さなブレークスルー

　2001年に入って間もないある夜、私とローナは、当時住んでいた北ロンドンの家の玄関側の一室を暗くして、ハワード・ホークス監督の1934年作品『特急二十世紀』を観はじめました。まずまずの画質のVHSビデオでした。映画のタイトルにある「二十世紀」とは、過ぎ去ったばかりの100年ではなく、世紀前半、ニューヨークとシカゴを結んでいた有名な豪華列車のことです。この映画をご存じの方もおられるでしょう。全篇ほぼ列車の中で展開するテンポのよいコメディです。ブロードウェイの主演級女優がハリウッドで映画スターになると言い出し、プロデューサーがなんとしてもこれを阻もうとします。見ものは、当時屈指の大俳優だったジョン・バリモアのコミカルな演技でしょう。表情、身振り手振り、言うセリフのほとんどすべて——そこに、自己中心的で自己顕示欲にとりつかれた男のアイロニー、矛盾、グロ

utters come layered with ironies, contradictions, the grotesqueries of a man drowning in egocentricity and self-dramatisation. It is in many ways a brilliant performance. Yet, as the film continued to unfold, I found myself curiously uninvolved. This puzzled me at first. I usually liked Barrymore, and was a big enthusiast for Howard Hawks's other films from this period – such as *His Girl Friday* and *Only Angels Have Wings*. Then, around the film's one-hour mark, a simple, striking idea came into my head. The reason why so many vivid, undeniably convincing characters in novels, films and plays so often failed to touch me was because these characters didn't connect to any of the other characters in an interesting human relationship. And immediately, this next thought came regarding my own work: What if I stopped worrying

テスクさが幾重にも込められています。いろいろな意味ですばらしい演技です。ですが、映画が進んでいくにつれ、私はなぜか画面にのめり込めないでいる自分に気づきました。最初は、あれっ、と思いました。いつもならバリモアは好きな俳優ですし、ハワード・ホークス監督のこの時代の作品——たとえば『ヒズ・ガール・フライデー』や『コンドル』など——の大ファンでもありましたから。やがて映画の始まりからちょうど1時間ほどしたころ、頭の中に単純で衝撃的な思いが浮かびました。小説でも映画でも演劇でもいい。生き生きと描かれ、確かにこういう人はいると思わせながら、なぜか琴線に触れてこない登場人物がいるのはなぜか。それは、その人物と他の登場人物との関係が、人間的つながりとして面白くないからではないか……。直後、自分自身の作品についてこんなことも思いました——登場人物についてあれこれ悩むかわりに、もっと人物間の関係について悩ん

about my characters and worried instead about my relationships?

As the train rattled farther west and John Barrymore became ever more hysterical, I thought about E.M. Forster's famous distinction between three-dimensional and two-dimensional characters. A character in a story became three-dimensional, he'd said, by virtue of the fact that they 'surprised us convincingly'. It was in so doing they became 'rounded'. But what, I now wondered, if a character was three-dimensional, while all his or her relationships were not? Elsewhere in that same lecture series, Forster had used a humorous image, of extracting the storyline out of a novel with a pair of forceps and holding it up, like a wriggling worm, for

でみたらどうだろう。

　列車がガタゴト西へ進み、ジョン・バリモアがいっそうヒステリックになっていくのを観ながら、私はＥ・Ｍ・フォースターの有名な二分法について考えていました。登場人物には立体的な人物と平面的な人物がいる、とフォースターは言います。そして、人物が「意外な動きをし、その意外さに読者が納得できれば」、その人物は「丸く（立体的に）」なっていく、と言います。しかし、と私は思いました。いくら登場人物が立体的であっても、その人物と他者との関係がまったく立体的でなかったらどうなるだろう……。同じ講義集のほかの場所で、フォースターは、鉗子を使って小説から筋を抜き出し、のたうつミミズか何かのようにそれを日の光のもとで観察する、というユーモラスなイメージを呈示しています。ど

examination under the light. Couldn't I perform a similar exercise and hold up to the light the various relationships that crisscross any story? Could I do this with my own work – to stories I'd completed and ones I was planning? I could look at, say, this mentor-pupil relationship. Does it say something insightful and fresh? Or now that I was staring at it, does it become obvious it's a tired stereotype, identical to those found in hundreds of mediocre stories? Or this relationship between two competitive friends: Is it dynamic? Does it have emotional resonance? Does it evolve? Does it surprise convincingly? Is it three-dimensional? I suddenly felt I understood better why in the past various aspects of my work had failed, despite my applying desperate remedies. The thought came to me – as I continued to stare at John Barrymore – that all

んな物語にもあれこれの人間関係が登場します。これも、同様にして日の光のもとにさらせないものだろうか、と私は考えました。自分の作品に――過去の作品と計画中の作品に――これをやってみたらどうだろう。たとえば、あの師弟関係をそうやって観察したら、何か深くて新しいことを語ってくれるだろうか。それとも、じろじろ見つめつづけるうち、ありきたりの凡百の物語同様、くたびれ切ったステレオタイプの正体をさらすだけだろうか。あっちの競い合う2人の友人関係はどうだろう。ダイナミックか。感情に響いてくるか。発展していきそうか。納得できる意外さを示せるか。立体的な関係か……。突然、私は、過去の作品のあの部分この部分について、なぜ失敗したのか――必死に手立てを講じたのに、なぜうまくいかなかったのか――がよくわかったように思いました。ジョン・バリモアを観つづける私の頭に、こんな考えが浮かんできました。語りの形式が突飛であれ伝統

good stories, never mind how radical or traditional their mode of telling, had to contain relationships that are important to us; that move us, amuse us, anger us, surprise us. Perhaps in future, if I attended more to my relationships, my characters would take care of themselves.

It occurs to me as I say this that I might be making a point here that has always been plainly obvious to you. But all I can say is that it was an idea that came to me surprisingly late in my writing life, and I see it now as a turning point, comparable with the others I've been describing to you today. From then on, I began to build my stories in a different way. When writing my novel *Never Let Me Go*, for instance, I set off from the start by thinking about its central relationships triangle, and

的であれ、すべてのすぐれた物語は、読者にとって重要と思える関係を——読者を衝き動かし、楽しませ、怒らせ、驚かす関係を——含んでいなければならない。これからはもっと関係に注意しよう。そうすれば、たぶん、登場人物が勝手に立体的になっていってくれるのではないか。

　いま私が新しい発見か何かのように語ったことは、皆さまにとってすでに自明のことだったかもしれません。いま、そう気づきました。そうだとすれば、あれは、私の作家人生の中で驚くほど遅れて来た発見だったということになります。いま振り返っても、あの夜がターニングポイントでした。今日ここまでお話ししてきたほかの出来事と比べても、勝るとも劣りません。あの夜以来、私は物語の組み立て方法を変えました。たとえば『わたしを離さないで』を書くとき、私はまず、中心となる三

then the other relationships that fanned out from it.

*

Important turning points in a writer's career – perhaps in many kinds of career – are like these. Often, they are small, scruffy moments. They are quiet, private sparks of revelation. They don't come often, and when they do, they may well come without fanfare, unendorsed by mentors or colleagues. They must often compete for attention with louder, seemingly more urgent demands. Sometimes what they reveal may go against the grain of prevailing wisdom. But when they come, it's important to be able to recognise

角関係から考えはじめ、次いで、そこから広がっていくはずのさまざまな関係を組み立てていきました。

*

　作家にとって重要なターニングポイントは——たぶん、多くの職業で同じかもしれませんが——こんなふうにやってきます。ちょっとした瞬間に、その人にだけわかる啓示の火花が静かに光ります。めったにあることではなく、あってもファンファーレつきとはかぎりません。お墨付きをくれる師や同僚もいないでしょう。その啓示と競い合うように、もっと声高に緊急の対応を要求してくる出来事があるかもしれませんし、啓示の意味することが時代の常識に反しているかもしれません。ですが、啓示を得たら、その何たるかを認識できることが重要です。

them for what they are. Or they'll slip through your hands.

I've been emphasising here the small and the private, because essentially that's what my work is about. One person writing in a quiet room, trying to connect with another person, reading in another quiet – or maybe not so quiet – room. Stories can entertain, sometimes teach or argue a point. But for me the essential thing is that they communicate feelings. That they appeal to what we share as human beings across our borders and divides. There are large, glamorous industries around stories; the book industry, the movie industry, the television industry, the theatre industry. But in the end, stories are about one person saying to another: This is the way it feels to me. Can you understand what

さもないと、せっかく来たものが手をすり抜けていってしまいます。

　ここでは、些細なこと、プライベートなことを述べてきました。作家の仕事とは本質的にそういうものだからです。1人が静かな部屋にいて、誰かとつながろうとして文章を書きます。別の静かな——いや、さほど静かでないかもしれませんね——部屋にいる誰かがそれを読みます。物語は読む人を楽しませ、ときに何事かを教え、議論を吹きかけます。しかし、物語ることの本質は、私にとっては何よりも感情を伝えることです。感情こそが境界線や隔壁を乗り越え、同じ人間として分かち合っている何かに訴えかけるものだからです。物語の周辺には、出版産業、映画産業、テレビ産業、演劇産業など、華やかな産業が群がっていますが、結局のところ、物語とは1人が別の1人にこう語りかけるものでしょう——私に

I'm saying? Does it also feel this way to you?

*

So we come to the present. I woke up recently to the realisation I'd been living for some years in a bubble. That I'd failed to notice the frustration and anxieties of many people around me. I saw that my world – a civilised, stimulating place filled with ironic, liberal-minded people – was in fact much smaller than I'd ever imagined. 2016, a year of surprising – and for me depressing – political events in Europe and in America, and of sickening acts of terrorism all around the globe, forced me to acknowledge that the unstoppable

はこう感じられるのですが、おわかりいただけるでしょうか？　あなたも同じように感じておられるでしょうか？

*

　さて、現在です。ここ何年か私は泡の中に生きてきたことに、最近気づきました。泡の中にいて、周囲の多くの人々の苛立ちや不安に気づかずにいたようです。私を取り巻く世界は教養と刺激にあふれ、リベラルな考えをもつ皮肉っぽい人々が集まっている世界です。しかし、それは想像していたよりずっと小さな世界だった、といま思います。2016年は、ヨーロッパとアメリカで驚くような——私には気の滅入るような——政治的出来事があった年でした。世界中で胸が悪くなりそうなテロ行為が頻発した年でもありました。私は子供のころから、リ

advance of liberal-humanist values I'd taken for granted since childhood may have been an illusion.

I'm part of a generation inclined to optimism, and why not? We watched our elders successfully transform Europe from a place of totalitarian regimes, genocide and historically unprecedented carnage to a much-envied region of liberal democracies living in near-borderless friendship. We watched the old colonial empires crumble around the world together with the reprehensible assumptions that underpinned them. We saw significant progress in feminism, gay rights and the battles on several fronts against racism. We grew up against a backdrop of the great clash – ideological and military – between capitalism and

ベラルで人道主義的な価値観を信じ、その広がりは止めようがないと信じてきましたが、それが幻想だったかもしれないと認めざるをえなくなりました。

　私の世代はともすると楽観主義に傾きがちです。ですが、それは当然のことでしょう。全体主義がはびこり、民族抹殺など、歴史上類を見ない大虐殺が横行していたヨーロッパを、年上の世代が見事に変身させるのを見てきましたから。結果、ヨーロッパは国境さえほぼなくし、友好関係に生きる自由民主主義の地という、誰もがうらやむ場所に変わりました。世界中の旧植民地帝国と、それを支えていた忌むべき思想が崩壊するのも見てきました。フェミニズムやゲイライツが進展し、人種差別との戦いが大きく前進するのを見てきました。資本主義と共産主義の思想的・軍事的衝突を背景にして育った私たちは、その衝突がハッピーエンド──と多くの人々が信じ

communism, and witnessed what many of us believed to be a happy conclusion.

But now, looking back, the era since the fall of the Berlin Wall seems like one of complacency, of opportunities lost. Enormous inequalities – of wealth and opportunity – have been allowed to grow, between nations and within nations. In particular, the disastrous invasion of Iraq in 2003, and the long years of austerity policies imposed on ordinary people following the scandalous economic crash of 2008, have brought us to a present in which Far Right ideologies and tribal nationalisms proliferate. Racism, in its traditional forms and in its modernised, better-marketed versions, is once again on the rise, stirring beneath our civilised streets like a buried monster

た結末——を迎えるのも目撃しました。

　しかし、いま振り返ってみると、ベルリンの壁が崩壊して以降、私たちはうぬぼれの時代、機会喪失の時代に入っていたのかもしれません。富と機会をめぐって、国内にも国家間にも大きな不平等が広がるのを見過ごしてしまいました。とりわけ、2003年には大失敗に終わったイラク侵攻がありましたし、2008年の経済恐慌以後には、長期間にわたる強制された緊縮政策によって庶民が苦しみました。極右思想や部族的ナショナリズムが跋扈する現在は、それらの結果として存在します。人種差別が——伝統的な形でも、売り込みやすい現代的な形でも——ふたたび勢いを盛り返す気配です。いま、埋もれていたモンスターのように、文明社会の大通りの下でうごめきはじめています。一方、私たちを一致団結させら

awakening. For the moment we seem to lack any progressive cause to unite us. Instead, even in the wealthy democracies of the West, we're fracturing into rival camps from which to compete bitterly for resources or power.

And around the corner – or have we already turned this corner? – lie the challenges posed by stunning breakthroughs in science, technology and medicine. New genetic technologies – such as the gene-editing technique CRISPR – and advances in Artificial Intelligence and robotics will bring us amazing, life-saving benefits, but may also create savage meritocracies that resemble apartheid, and massive unemployment, including to those in the current professional elites.

れる進歩的な大義は、まだ見えてきていません。西欧の裕福な民主主義国でさえ、人々は分裂し、いくつもの敵対的陣営に分かれて、資力や権力を争い合っています。

　科学技術や医療の分野で従来の壁を破る発見が相次ぎ、そこから派生する脅威の数々が、すぐそこまでやって来ています。いや、もう到着しているでしょうか。CRISPRのような新しい遺伝子編集技術が編み出され、人工知能やロボット技術にも大きな進展があります。それは人命救助というすばらしい利益をもたらしてくれますが、同時に、アパルトヘイトにも似た野蛮な能力主義社会を出現させ、いまはまだエリートとみなされている専門職の人々をも巻き込む、大量失業時代を招くかもしれません。

So here I am, a man in my sixties, rubbing my eyes and trying to discern the outlines, out there in the mist, to this world I didn't suspect even existed until yesterday. Can I, a tired author, from an intellectually tired generation, now find the energy to look at this unfamiliar place? Do I have something left that might help to provide perspective, to bring emotional layers to the arguments, fights and wars that will come as societies struggle to adjust to huge changes?

I'll have to carry on and do the best I can. Because I still believe that literature is important, and will be particularly so as we cross this difficult terrain. But I'll be looking to the writers from the younger generations

特急二十世紀の夜と、いくつかの小さなブレークスルー

　60歳を超えた私は、いまかすむ目をこすりながら見定めようとしています。昨日までその存在にすら気づかなかった世界の輪郭はどんなでしょうか。それはまだ霧の中にあってぼんやりしています。知的に疲弊した世代の疲弊した作家である私は、この未知の世界をじっと見据えるのに必要なエネルギーを見つけられるでしょうか。社会が巨大な変化に適応しようとするとき、議論や争いや戦いが起こります。そんな争いに新しい見方を与え、感情をともなわせるための一助となる何かが、私にまだ残されているでしょうか。

　私は投げ出さず、最善を尽くさなければならないでしょう。なぜなら、文学は重要であると——この困難な地平を渡っていくためにはいっそう重要であると——私は信じているからです。若い世代の作家が頼りです。若い

to inspire and lead us. This is their era, and they will have the knowledge and instinct about it that I will lack. In the worlds of books, cinema, TV and theatre I see today adventurous, exciting talents: women and men in their forties, thirties and twenties. So I am optimistic. Why shouldn't I be?

But let me finish by making an appeal – if you like, my Nobel appeal! It's hard to put the whole world to rights, but let us at least think about how we can prepare our own small corner of it, this corner of 'literature', where we read, write, publish, recommend, denounce and give awards to books. If we are to play an important role in this uncertain future, if we are to get the best from the writers of today and tomorrow, I believe we

人々が私たちに閃きを与え、導いてくれることを願っています。これは彼らの時代です。来る(きた)べき世界について、私にはない知識と本能を備えています。本、映画、テレビ、演劇のどの分野にも、冒険心に富んだすばらしい才能が——40代、30代、20代の男女が——ひしめいています。私は楽観的です。楽観的であってならない理由がありません。

　最後に一つの呼びかけを——僭越ながらノーベル賞受賞者からの呼びかけを——お許しください。この世界の全体を正すことは困難です。ならば、せめて本を読み、書き、出版し、推薦し、批判し、授賞しつづけられるよう、私たちの住むこの「文学」という小さな一角だけでも、維持発展させていきましょう。不確かな未来に私たちが何か意味ある役割を果たしていくつもりなら——今日と明日の作家から、それぞれのベストを引き出そうと

must become more diverse. I mean this in two particular senses.

Firstly, we must widen our common literary world to include many more voices from beyond our comfort zones of the elite first-world cultures. We must search more energetically to discover the gems from what remain today unknown literary cultures, whether the writers live in faraway countries or within our own communities. Second, we must take great care not to set too narrowly or conservatively our definitions of what constitutes good literature. The next generation will come with all sorts of new, sometimes bewildering ways to tell important and wonderful stories. We must keep our minds open to them, especially regarding genre and form, so that we can nurture and celebrate

願うなら——私たちはもっと多様にならなければなりません。私の言う「多様」の意味は２つです。

　第１に、共通の文学的世界を広げていくことです。先進国のエリート文化という居心地のいい枠内にとどまらず、外からの声を取り込むことです。未知の文学をもつ文化を積極的に探し、そこから宝石を掘り出してくることです。それは遠くの国にいる作家かもしれませんし、同じ町内の作家かもしれません。第２に、よい文学の定義です。何がすぐれた文学かを考えるとき、あまりに狭い保守的な議論は避けるよう十分な注意が必要です。次世代の作家は、ありとあらゆる新しい表現方法で——ときには頭が混乱するような方法で——重要な話、すばらしい話を語ろうとするでしょう。とくにジャンルと様式については、心をオープンに保ち、現れてくる最良のものを祝福し、育まなければなりません。亀裂が危険なほ

the best of them. In a time of dangerously increasing division, we must listen. Good writing and good reading will break down barriers. We may even find a new idea, a great humane vision, around which to rally.

To the Swedish Academy, the Nobel Foundation and to the people of Sweden who down the years have made the Nobel Prize a shining symbol for the good we human beings strive for – I give my thanks.

ど拡大している時代だからこそ、耳を澄ませる必要があります。よい作品を書き、よい作品を読むことで、障壁が打ち破られます。その過程で新しい思想が現れ、スケールの大きな人道的構想が練られて、私たちの結集を促すかもしれません。

　スウェーデン・アカデミーの皆さま、ノーベル財団の皆さま、長年にわたってノーベル賞を人類が目指す善なるものの輝く象徴にしてくださったスウェーデン国民の皆さま、心より感謝します。

訳者略歴　英米文学翻訳家　訳書『日の名残り』『わたしを離さないで』『忘れられた巨人』カズオ・イシグロ，『エデンの東』ジョン・スタインベック（以上早川書房刊），『イギリス人の患者』マイケル・オンダーチェ，他多数

とっきゅうにじっせいき　　　　よる
特急二十世紀の夜と、
　　　　　　　　　　　ちい
いくつかの小さなブレークスルー
ノーベル文学賞受賞記念講演

2018年2月10日　初版印刷
2018年2月15日　初版発行

著　者　カズオ・イシグロ
　　　　　　つちやまさお
訳　者　土屋政雄
発行者　早川　浩
印刷所　精文堂印刷株式会社
製本所　大口製本印刷株式会社
発行所　株式会社　早川書房
郵便番号　101-0046
東京都千代田区神田多町2-2
電話　03-3252-3111（大代表）
振替　00160-3-47799
http://www.hayakawa-online.co.jp

ISBN978-4-15-209747-7 C0098
定価はカバーに表示してあります。
Printed and bound in Japan

乱丁・落丁本は小社制作部宛お送り下さい。
送料小社負担にてお取りかえいたします。
本書のコピー、スキャン、デジタル化等の無断複製は
著作権法上の例外を除き禁じられています。